The first book in the *London Deep* series was chosen as a R   *ed Read* for *World Book Day* 2011 and as one of the *Man-* ch   *Award's* 24 recommended reads for 2010.

'I   rifically atmospheric page-turning adventure told through w   comic art... a rattling good read and one in which you are su   drawn in to Jem's exploits of survival.' – *Lovereading.co.uk*

'I   pace and narrative power, both admirably sustained, the b   ds becoming didactic. This is no campaign document on cl   nge... The characterization, especially of Jemima and N   ceful and convincing. They capture the reader's interest ar   he narrative forward...' – *Armadillo Magazine*

'R   ce's writing is quirky with a bit of an edge to it that greatly ac   n to this dystopian version of London... Add in the gritty ill   comic panels by Paul McGrory and you find this is indeed som   g quite new, not only in plot, but in style...with the comic pane   ding punctuation to the action occurring within that part of the cha   r.' – *Dooyoo.co.uk*

'Is this   art graphic novel, part standard text, or is it a story with illustrat   s...? ... My eleven year old loved it and seemed to have no trouble cutting backwards and forwards between the two...' – Rachel Ayers Nelson, *School Librarian Magazine*

'London Deep is a really amazing story about a twelve year old girl called Jemima Mallard. She lives in a flooded London of the future!! ... This book is a very enjoyable read with lots of drama action and fun. The comic pics are very enjoyable to look at and   kind of story.' – Abigail (aged 10)

FATHER THAMES

MOGZILLA

Father Thames

First published by Mogzilla in 2011

Paperback edition:

ISBN: 9781906132040

Printed in the UK

www.mogzilla.co.uk/fatherthames

www.paulmcgrory.co.uk

Paul would like to thank the following people:

Jim, Carol, Kathy, Rachel, Jane Stobart, Graham, Charlie, Jane, Jess, Bob & Elizabeth, Adam, Debbie, Joseph, Paul, Tom, Clarky, Jack, Katie and Andy.

Robin would like to thank the following people:

Michele, Peter, Rachel, Jess, Alex, John and Barbera, Nic and Scarlet.

Recap

Father Thames is set in the near future in a flooded London where rival police forces for kids and grown ups compete to keep the peace.

Jemima Mallard lived on a houseboat with her father, a Chief Inspector in the APD (Adult Police Department). One morning, Jem broke so many laws that even her father's diplomacy couldn't get her out of trouble. Arrested by a YPD (Youth Police Department) officer called Nick, she made a bargain. In exchange for a full pardon, she agreed to help the YPD track down a criminal organisation called *Father Thames*, only to discover that her own mother was one of its leaders! These 'terrorists' were drilling for gas under the river Thames. When Jem and her mother met, sparks flew and her mother's friend, nicknamed 'The Fatman,' paid the price.

Jem refused her mum's invitation to join Father Thames, and decided to join the YPD instead. This is what happened next....

Assembly

THE YPD'S SUPREME MANDER ADDRESSED HIS NEW RECRUITS.

THERE'S ENOUGH ROOM IN THE DEAR OLD TOWER FOR EVERY CHILD WHO CHOOSES THE WRONG PATH.

LET'S HOPE THAT TOWER IS BIG ENOUGH - I'M GONNA MEET MY TARGETS!

WITH US ON THE CASE WE'LL BE NEEDING A NEW BLOODY TOWER!

BUT REMEMBER, IF THE CRIME INVOLVES THE OVER-AGED, IT'S YOUR DUTY TO STAND DOWN.

REMEMBER...

DO NOT GET INVOLVED WITH GREY-CRIME. LEAVE IT TO THE APD.

'Down with the 'Dults!' came the cry. The chant was sucked up to the rafters and it bounced back off the ceiling to the ranks below. The rivalry between the police forces for kids and grown-ups was legendary. Most of the recruits took up the old feud with vigour, but not every YPD officer ran with the pack.

Jemima Mallard sniggered uncontrollably.

'Check out the Mander in his new hat. It's REALLY pointy!'

'I could look at him all day. He's kind of cute,' giggled her friend Celine.

'I suppose he is,' replied Jem. 'If you're into authoritarians.'

'They should've let me design the uniforms,' said Celine. 'I was going to be a clothes designer like my dad, before I joined up.'

Jem practically exploded with laughter.

'The Young Fashion Police! Brownshirts are the new black! And this season, riot truncheons are long...'

'Sshhhhh!' snorted the tall recruit to their left.

'For Lud's sake! Show some respect!' came a call from behind.

One of the Wave Commanders would normally have pulled them out of line for talking in the ranks and put them on a charge. Luckily for Jemima, there wasn't room in the hall to wave a charge sheet. Besides, after months of lectures, practicals and on-water training, high spirits were to be expected.

It was traditional for the Mander to address the recruits each year at graduation, and every time there was a new theme. The YPD loved its slogans, and the adult police weren't much better. Jem wondered what the Thames's hardened criminals would think if they knew they were being busted as part of the 'Scupper Crime' initiative or 'Operation Seaslug' or whatever bizarre name they'd come up. Poor Jem! She was doing her best, but she often wondered if she had the right personality for Youth Police work.

The Mander raised his baton and called for silence.

Haig, the Head of Psyc Ops, stood next to the Mander,

peering out at the crowd. Jem wasn't the only one with the feeling that behind his regulation sunglasses, Haig's eyes were on her.

Young people matter

YOUNG PEOPLE MATTERED TO JEMIMA MALLARD ALL RIGHT. Before she'd even finished her training at Hendon Marsh, she'd started hunting down her mother's little helpers.

Jem was furious that her mum had walked out on her seven long years ago. 'Rage' didn't really get close to describing how she felt. It was so bad that she'd have arrested her own mother if it were legal – which of course it wasn't. Her mum was over the age limit. So Jem had made it her business to track down every young member of her mum's terrorist group – Father Thames. Maybe 'terrorists' wasn't the right word for them. Apart from a little illegal gas prospecting, the most criminal thing about them was their taste in boiler suits and the way they went through electricity like water. Hadn't they ever heard of the Climate Upgrade?

That evening, after the rally, it was back to the usual routine.

Nick liked Jem – really liked her. He'd been assigned to 'mentor' her when she'd joined up so unexpectedly. They'd become room-mates and Rudi, Nick's not-so-faithful attack dog, had been banished to the kennels. Nick's interest in Jem had crept up on him and now it was so bad that thinking about her was starting to disrupt his precious routines. Unfilled intel forms lay around the place, some of his treasured equipment was left unserviced. Not that he'd ever dare say anything to Jemima. Nick never had anything to say to girls, unless he was arresting them of course.

Soon after he started noticing Jem, he also noticed that his new room mate was obsessed with Father Thames and spent most of her free nights reading about them. The paperwork was illegal, 'borrowed' from the APD. Jem was giving it the sort of attention that gets you a note on your record, a visit from Psyc Ops, or a promotion to Wave Commander.

Jem didn't understand. Most mums had hobbies, like a book circle or a fishing club but hers had joined a terrorist cell.

For Jem, it was beyond personal: she'd joined the YPD solely in order to get herself assigned to counter-terrorist duties.

JEM SET ABOUT TRACKING DOWN FATHER THAMES.

ASIF HAD BEEN THE EASIEST.

JAMIL PUT UP A DECENT FIGHT.

NOW THEY WERE AFTER THE LAST ONE...

Plume

THE GIRL, SHAMI, WAS SLIPPERY. They'd come close to capturing her a couple of times but come away empty handcuffed. What was the phrase Nick had used? 'The suspect is highly adapt at evasion.'

This time they had a lead from an informant on a steamer by the Socket, (what was left of the old London Eye). The ruined wheel was part monument and part navigational aid. Ships would moor up next to it for trading because it was hard to find safe anchorage in the open river. Jem was day-dreaming through her shift, when she spotted a black plume rising in the still air.

Nick wound up the radio and called it in. Even petty crimes counted towards his arrest stats. He hoped and prayed that it was kids! There were still a few idiots clueless enough to flout the emissions regs. The Controller's voice answered, with a crackle:

'Copy that Aqua 3. What is the source of the pollution?'

'Let's leave it Nick,' sighed Jem, still hoping to follow up the lead on Shami. 'It's probably some old granny burning her dinner.'

'It's coming from the east, from Sector 7P.'

'Investigate and report Aqua 3,' came the order.

'Copy that,' muttered Jem, with little enthusiasm.

'Sector 7P,' said Nick. 'Isn't that a penal sector?'

Two miles down river, a guard peered out from the bridge connecting the twin towers of the YPD prison. A chill wind rushed down the face of the tower and knifed through his uniform. Being a guard had been fun when he used to play camps with his older brothers, but in reality it meant empty hours on lonely walkways.

'Hey!' he cried. Far below, a fleet of unusual craft had appeared. 'Look at that! D'you think the Whale Roaders are in town?'

'Nah. Can't be!' said the second guard, spitting for emphasis. The ball of spittle fell 20 metres down to the water's surface.

'They've disbanded. Probably just B-Tower on an exercise.'

The last thing he heard was the zing of grappling hooks snagging on the gantry before a flaming arrow found its mark.

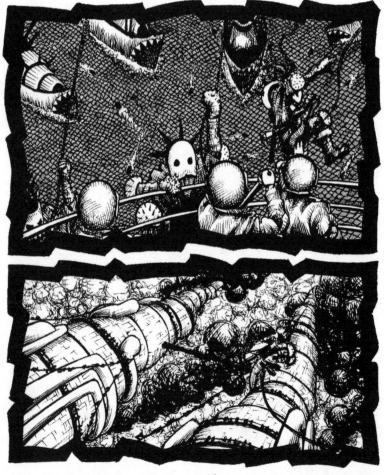

Back on the Aqua, Jem could taste the smoke that billowed out in tall plumes as they drew nearer to the Tower. There were no cries on the rising wind and only acrid fumes filled the silence.

Whenever the subject of 'Father Thames' came up, Nick's partner went all distant. Her obsession had been great for his arrest stats as it had led to three major busts in as many months.

However, Jem's behaviour was getting compulsive – she was worse than his dog Rudi when he got his teeth into a tyre. Making a mental note not to share that image with Jemima, Nick cut the engine and they glided up to one of the stragglers of the unidentified fleet.

'We'll call it in to HQ,' answered Nick, frantically winding up the radio. 'We can't take an enemy ship single handed.'

'How do we know they're our enemies?' asked Jem.

'You're right!' said Nick. 'Perhaps they were out on a picnic cruise and they set fire to our major penal facility by accident?'

For a girl who scored A++ in her 'Intelligence' unit, Jem certainly said some silly things sometimes.

'Let's leave it and call it in on the way back,' suggested Jem.

Nick stared at the girl in amazement. This was it! Their first chance to put their counter-terrorist training to the test – and Jem simply couldn't be bothered.

'What's up with you today Ms Mallard?' he enquired.

'Sorry,' said Jem. 'It's those decals on the prow. Sharks kind of creep me out. And besides, there's that promising lead on Shami.'

Nick smiled. So that was it! Her pet project again. Well, the last member of her mother's gang would have to wait this time.

He'd prepared his grappling iron so he was disappointed to find a perfectly good ladder running up the side of the ship.

'Stay put if you don't feel confident,' said Nick, handing Jem the radio. 'If I'm not back in 10 minutes, summon assistance.'

Waiting for a wave to bring him in close, Nick got a good hold of the ship's ladder, stepped across and began to climb.

Jem looked up at the unknown vessel, cradling the radio.

Relatively few things disturbed Jemima Mallard. Apart from sharks, (not an irrational fear as far as Jem was concerned), her other weakness were a dislike of high places and any kind of climbing (and ladders in particular). However, moments later, she found herself stepping onto the first of the steel rungs.

'Stay put if you don't feel confident!' she muttered. The ascent was challenging and her muscles began to burn so much that the top of the ladder was a welcome sight. Jem hauled herself aboard to find the deck deserted and the wind rising.

'A ghost ship!' said Jem. 'Nice!'

The atmosphere was no better below deck. All the corridors led to a hollow central space, where sets of iron chains were arranged in neat rows. Jem shuddered at the sight of the shackles.

LOOKS LIKE THE DOGS ARE LOOSE.

An unexpected cry boomed around the empty space. Looking up, she spotted two shapes in the shadows near the door. A tall figure was leading another shape by a rope. She gasped. The smaller one obviously had some kind of deformity. It was wrong to stare, but her eyes were drawn to its big bug eyes and ragged teeth. To her relief she realised that the tall figure was Nick.

'Jem!' he called. 'I thought you were staying put.'

Jem didn't answer, her eyes were still glued to the creature.

'Found anything then?' asked Nick, seemingly unphased that he had caught a devil, or a troll or whatever it was, and was leading it about on a rope. 'I found this one skulking around below deck.'

Jem breathed a second sigh of relief when she realised that Nick's captive was wearing a mask.

Jem shook her head disapprovingly. She'd been brought up to be sympathetic to foreigners, even though she'd never met one.

'Good job! They all speak English, if you threaten them.'

Nick groaned. This girl had a flair for making him feel stupid.

'Let's get a look at you,' said Jem, reaching to undo the mask.

Gently, Jem removed the mask.

Freefalling

EVERY TOWER MUST FALL SOMEDAY. The shouts rang from pen to pen and from cell to cell. The 'Bloody Tower', the YPD's most feared prison was falling to the invaders. Grim-faced guards huddled in the smoke, some with tear-tracks streaking their grimy faces. They had never predicted an onslaught like this and they could only watch as the raiders blew through their defences and the masks danced amongst them.

Battleship chains

IN AN AIRLESS ROOM BACK AT HENDON MARSH, THE MANDER PUSHED HIS MODELS AROUND THE OPERATIONS BOARD. One of the little ships toppled over, but he set it upright using his baton.

The YPD's chief commander had confident eyes and an easy manner with his staff that made them feel valued. Yet under the mask of leadership, he was concerned. He'd prepared a few words for the officers gathered in his ready room, but when he saw Haig enter, he decided to cut the speech and get down to business.

Before Haig could finish his report, a flustered officer crashed through the door and stood before him, puffing apologetically.

'Do you like penguins?' asked Haig. His voice wasn't exactly 'cold' but it had an empty quality; all its expression got lost in the back of Haig's throat. Even his personal staff often found it hard to tell whether their commander was satisfied or furious. In short, it was the perfect voice for the Head of Psyc Ops, (the elite intelligence division that Haig commanded).

'Sorry sir?' said the confused officer.

'It's Sergeant Bates isn't it?'

Bates nodded.

'I hope you appreciate penguins Bates,' said Haig. 'Because you'll be sent to Anglesea to live with them permanently if you ever interrupt me again.'

The unfortunate officer apologised for the second time.

'There's been a call from the 'Dult Police on the scrambled channel. Did we know that our prison is on fire?'

All eyes fell on the Mander.

'Sergeant, thank the APD for their concern and confirm that we are aware of the situation,' he said.

Bates moved towards the exit but the Mander stopped him.

'Stay for this Sergeant, we're having a heads up session. Now, here's the puzzle – why would raiders attack a prison? There are no resources there. Nothing at all of any value.'

No one spoke.

'All opinions and ideas are welcome,' said the Mander. 'Sometimes the smallest voices have the biggest ideas,' was a saying of his. But not this time...

'It might be the Bargers rioting?' said the Mander's assistant.

'Maybe it's the 'Dults,' said Bates, 'no one's attacking them.'

This thought had crossed the Mander's mind already but the reports said the attackers were a 'mixed-aged force'. Besides, the APD would have little to gain from an escalation of tension.

The Mander felt he should say something incisive but he was stumped. 'When there are no answers, ask better questions' was another one of his sayings.

'It might be foreigners sir,' suggested his assistant. 'There's nowhere you can hide a fleet like that without Psyc Ops knowing about it. So they must have come through the Barrier Sir.'

'Impossible sir! Those chains are strong enough to stop a battleship.'

'Yet here they are,' said the Mander.

'We think they must have used countermeasures, Sir.'

The Mander took up his baton and pointed it at Haig.

'Come on then. What's the intel? You must have ideas.'

The Head of Psyc Ops rocked back in his chair and began explaining in a matter-of-fact manner:

'At about 6am, the first raiding party got out of their boat and lifted it over the chains. Then they scaled the wall and broke into the Barrier control room, securing it without resistance. It was then a straightforward matter to lower the chains, and let the rest of their fleet through.'

The Mander brought his baton down on the table, scattering the models like dandelion seed.

Konami

SORRY ABOUT THE SUPRISE JEMIMA. TELL JUNIOR HERE TO UNTIE ME.

TELL HIM YOURSELF MOTHER HIS NAME'S NICK. YOU'VE ALREADY MET HIM, REMEMBER?

Nick looked from mother to child and back again – the resemblance was striking. River, Jem's mum, was an older, sulkier version of her daughter, (if the latter was possible).

'You ought to know the age-law by now Jemima,' said River, 'since you've been studying it with such zeal.'

Nick could hear the disappointment in her voice.

'I'm over-age, so you're making a false arrest.'

The two YPD officers knew that, however frustrating it might be, River was right.

Jem eyed her mother like a young cat that had caught its first rat and didn't know quite what to do next.

'Hey Nick! As this perp is over-age, why don't we call our liaison officer in the Dult Police. Maybe we can release her to their anti-terrorist unit?'

Nick was a bit taken aback by this suggestion of colluding with the APD, but he actually gave it some thought.

Although the idea was appealing, Nick remembered his Mander's voice from the rally: 'Do not get involved in grey crime. Leave that to the APD.'

Were Father Thames behind this latest attack? Even if he couldn't arrest River himself, he might be able to get some vital information out of her. Jem fixed her mother with a glare, evidently she was following the same line of enquiry.

Before Nick could find out what River meant by this remark, the radio crackled into life again.

'YPD units! YPD units! CODE: KONAMI. CODE: KONAMI.'

Nick nearly dropped the handset in shock.

'Konami,' he said, recovering his composure. 'Know what that means Jem?'

Jem shook her head, not registering the shock in his voice.

'Code names, oh joy!' she muttered. 'Go on , since you're simply dying to tell me. What does 'KONAMI' mean when it's afloat?'

Before Nick could answer, there was a sudden jolt and a rumble like giant's teeth grinding. The deck lurched violently, sending the three of them flying towards the rail.

Nick was the first to get back to his feet. He eyed River suspiciously, anticipating an escape attempt.

There was a second jolt. This time Nick managed to keep his balance but a wave of cold spray came over the handrail and soaked his newly polished boots.

'Don't take your eyes off your mother Jem,' he warned.

Nick moved over to the rail and peered intently through the shrouds of smoke. He started fumbling with the case of his field-glasses, but you didn't need optics for what he was about to witness. He heard River's voice behind him, soft but serious.

Fire

Sᴇʀɢᴇᴀɴᴛ Bᴀᴛᴇs ʀᴜsʜᴇᴅ ᴛᴏᴡᴀʀᴅs ᴛʜᴇ ʀᴇᴀᴅʏ ʀᴏᴏᴍ ᴅᴏᴏʀ, ᴛʜᴏᴜɢʜᴛ ᴀʙᴏᴜᴛ ᴘᴇɴɢᴜɪɴs, ᴀɴᴅ ᴋɴᴏᴄᴋᴇᴅ ɴᴇʀᴠᴏᴜsʟʏ ʙᴇꜰᴏʀᴇ ʜᴇ ᴇɴᴛᴇʀᴇᴅ.

The operations board in front of the Mander was empty now. Since every YPD craft had been captured, disabled or sunk; it seemed best to clear away the evidence of failure.

'What is it?' said the Mander wearily, not turning to face him.

Bates approached with caution.

'The APD want to meet us Sir. Apparently, they've come under attack too. Their High Chief Constable is on route by jetski.'

'It must have cost a few litres of bio to move that fat old fossil on a 'ski,' laughed the Mander.

'HCC Greeves was purged last year,' said Haig. 'His replacement is a petite woman called Ohara.'

Over in Sector 7P, the fighting was nearly over.

As the order to 'Reload!' came, the cannon was already rolling backwards on the rails with wisps of grey smoke slipping from its iron mouth. A man in a mask grabbed two woollen bags and set them inside. He patted the gun lovingly on the belly, in the way that you might pet a cat. A woman not older than twenty rolled the iron ball down the barrel and the gunner rammed it home.

'One more to finish them?' asked the woman.

'No need,' smiled the man. 'Get ready with the nets. This lot are ours for the taking.'

Billy Ruffian

Nick lowered the field glasses in amazement and then raised them again for a second look. The wooden ship approaching was crewed by an assortment of masked warriors, their cloaks flapping in the breeze, just like an image from a historypod. This was simply incredible – only the bitter gunsmoke made it believable.

Jem glared at her prisoner, unfazed by the bizarre sight in the water before her. Her relationship with her mother was a bit like one long negotiation, and the pauses were important. A well-placed silence could give one side or the other the upper-hand.

'Tell us first mother, then we'll untie your hands,' offered Jem.

Nick shook his head in disbelief. 'One of yours?' he asked.

They had to call this in and get back to the Aqua fast.

'Let's go!' he ordered, 'Talk while you walk please ladies.'

As they reached the ladder a nearby launch burst into flames. Jem was dreading the long climb down. She was scared, but she was hiding it well.

'As I've just explained, *The Billy Ruffian* is the name of that flagship Jemima,' said River.

'Stop calling me Jemima!' snapped Jem, furious that her mum had found a way of annoying her with the sound of her own name.

It was a struggle to free River's hands but the climb down to the Aqua was tricky, so they'd have to trust her for now. Nick left the rope around her shoulders, just in case.

By the end of the descent, Jem wasn't even close to running out of silly remarks about pirates.

'Mum,' said Jem seriously. 'There's just one more thing. Please, it's really important.'

A stray shot hit the water nearby and set the Aqua rocking.

'But I hear they like to keep some of the old traditions going,' said River without missing a beat.

Nick hauled the starter cord but the motor only spluttered.

Nick pulled the starter cord for a final time but it was hopeless, his pride and joy certainly picked its moments to fail.

'Don't do that! You'll flood it,' snapped Jem, newly armed with knowledge from the unit on Mechanics she'd passed recently.

The prow of the *Billy Ruffian* glided into sight.

'They've seen us,' cried Jem, 'let's go!'

'Now would be good please officers, they're lowering a boat,' added River.

Nick cursed, frantically hauling on the starter. River picked up the mask from the floor and started to put it back on.

'I'd take that mask off,' Nick advised. 'In a hostage situation, you should make low-level eye contact with the kidnappers.'

Puppet show

HAIG AND THE MANDER WERE BAKING IN THE READY-ROOM. The fans had all wound down and the Mander wished someone would rewind them, but felt that he shouldn't be the one to give the order.

That devil Haig seemed to thrive in the heat and the darkness.

'Well Haig, what's the latest intel from Psyc Ops?'

Haig sat back down in the chair and studied his leader's face.

'We're not certain. They could have come looking for oil or... another power source. Maybe they're just lucky opportunists?'

'That's not all though, it is Haig?' asked the Mander.

Haig's voice dropped to the lowest of whispers.

'One of our Operators has a theory...' he began.

'Go on,' demanded the Mander, eagerly.

'The exact phrase that he used was "Religiously motivated."'

Haig wondered how long he could go on with this pretence.

You didn't need to be the head of Psyc Ops to know that image was crucial. The research showed that children liked a tall leader with a kind, symmetrical face. The younger ones responded well to a 'fatherly' voice which spoke with authority without being aggressive. Admittedly, they hadn't planned the scar, but it added a dash of danger. To balance this, they'd added a note of compassion to his profile. The leader must pay each one of them personal attention and care. Even the word 'Mander' looked similar to the word 'mother' when it was written down.

However sound this reasoning, Haig was growing tired of his puppet. He envied the showmen on the circus boats that came sailing into town – they didn't have to brief Punch and Judy twice a day as well as operate them.

'The intel points at some kind of hostile culture that wants to invade us – perhaps for mystical or religious reasons.'

'Mystic pirates?' said the Mander. 'That's hardly credible.'

'Perhaps not, but our Operator found certain signs at the scene,' replied Haig, producing a viewer from his coat pocket.

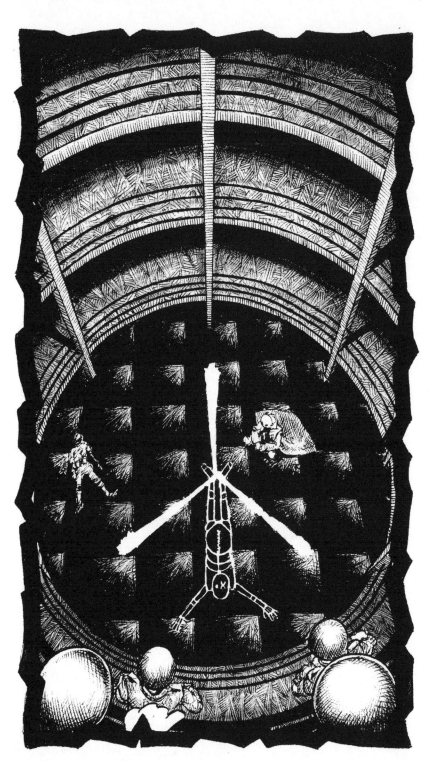

The device came alive, pixels glowing on its forbidden screen.

'What was that figure?' gasped the Mander in horror.

'Who knows. Some kind of ritual inscription,' said Haig.

'I meant the figure doing the painting,' said the Mander. 'The one in the mask.'

Haig shrugged.

'Our Operator only had the chance to take one more picture.'

Checking behind him, he leaned in and whispered something in the Mander's ear. Then he handed him the Viewer.

'Excuse me sir. Can I come in?' asked Bates, wondering how many penguins lived in a colony as he waited at the doorway.

'Leave us!' screamed Haig, shaking with rage as he scooped the Viewer off the desk and concealed it under his coat.

'Sorry Sir! It can't wait!' spluttered the frightened sergeant.

'What is it Bates?' asked the Mander patiently.

'I'm afraid we need to evacuate you Sir. This area isn't secure.'

Keep it safe

THE AQUA'S ANCIENT MOTOR WAS HISTORY.

'They've definitely lowered a boat,' said River through the gaping mouth hole in the war-mask. 'I can hear an outboard.'

'What now Nick?' called Jem, but her partner was still locked in mortal combat with the engine.

Jem turned to her mother – the swagger had drained from her expression, leaving a concerned pout.

She wondered why her mother needed to hide from the attackers? Other girl's mums wore jewellery, hers was in a war-mask trying to out-stare an enemy flagship.

'Nick?' Jem shouted again but he didn't answer. 'Nick! For Lud's sake, leave that now and get out the diving gear!'

Cursing the antique engine, Nick pulled the front panel of a hatch under the floor of the stern, dragged out a holdall and emptied its contents into a pile.

'Where's the rest of the gear?' demanded Jem in a panic, Nick didn't answer. 'There's more diving kit somewhere around here, right?' she cried.

Nick shook his head. The second mask set was back in the workshops being calibrated. What was wrong with him? He was well known for being obsessive about procedure; back at Hendon Marsh, they joked that he filled in a permission slip before brushing his teeth every morning. Yet inexplicably, he'd gone out on patrol without doing the proper equipment checks.

'I'm sorry,' he said flatly. There's only one mask,'

'Don't worry dears, I've got mine on already,' said River.

Jem stared at her mother in disbelief.

'But Mum, I'm a trained free-diver, they want me to sit the exam for instructor next year. You take the respirator, I'll dive down and hide under the boat and then surface when it's safe.'

The mask moved slowly from side to side.

'Get changed darling.'

'But mother...' began Jem as her mum helped her out of the heavy overalls.

'Don't worry. Don't descend too fast. And take this.'

River pressed a small cloth bundle into Jem's shaking hand.

'What is it?' asked Jem. But her mother didn't answer. Without thinking, Jem zipped it into the pocket of her under suit.

'Please keep this safe Jemima. It means a lot to me, I want you to keep it,' said River.

Putting her arms on Jem's shoulders, she edged back towards the side of the boat.

'Now hit me,' she said.

'What?' gasped Jem.

'Quickly! We've got to make this look convincing,' said River.

Nick clocked Jemima's puzzled expression and explained.

'We're going to pretend to be your mother's prisoners. She'll be escorting us back to their flagship but we'll jump her and escape.'

'Precisely,' said River. 'Now go ahead and hit me Jemima.'

'Do as she says. Swing your arm round in an arc so that it's clearly visible from their boat,' suggested Nick. 'Don't hit her too hard,' he added.

'Thanks,' said River. 'I hope I'll do the same for you one day.'

Jem pulled her arm right back and swung at her mother's masked face. As the punch connected, River was already pushing off with her legs and throwing herself backwards over the side.

'Let's go,' called Nick, not waiting to watch River hit the water. 'Stay close!' he said, clutching the air tank and respirator in one arm and taking Jem by the other.

Nick held Jem's hand as the pair dropped off the back of the Aqua and sank into the grey Thames.

The cold water stung Jem's face. Through her goggles, she could see thousands of tiny domes clinging to their bodies as they sank. Now she knew what it felt like to be inside a bursting bubble.

Suddenly she let go of Nick's hand.

Nick pawed around in a panic, searching for the girl. He peered around in every direction but there was nothing to be seen but murky water.

Everything was going wrong! First they'd lost River and now he'd managed to lose Jem as well. He took a slug of air from the mouthpiece and kicked for the surface as quickly as he dared.

Gone

'For fill's sake! Where's she gone?' cried Nick as he surfaced in the middle of a patch of sticky green algae.

Thankfully he had the sense to look around or the raiders would surely have spotted him. Fortunately for Nick they had their minds on another catch and they cruised straight past him.

'Jem!' he cried, rising on a small swell whipped up by the east wind. Caution soon drove him underwater again. Since he couldn't overpower an enemy boat, logic told him to dive down, wait it out for a few minutes and then swim to the nearest Keep. The YPD holding pens were fitted with radio equipment so he could call for help. When he surfaced for the second time, the raiders and their flagship had faded into nondescript dots on the horizon.

After an hour in the water with only the gulls for company, it was clear that finding a Keep wasn't an option. The watery horizon sucked the perspective out of everything, he might even have floated past one already without spotting it.

Nick had rehearsed for situations like this and he'd even memorised chunks of the YPD survival manual. There was a whole chapter on 'prolonged submersion' – your best strategy was to save your energy and flag down a passing vessel. Of course, the manual didn't say anything about enemy craft. There was a separate chapter in the Tactics manual about 'evading the enemy' but nothing that combined the two. Maybe Jem was right, 'normal' people don't read manuals because they're useless.

He was swimming on his back when he spotted the familiar outline of a YPD launch upside down against the stormy summer sky. Overjoyed, he tried to signal to it. For a horrible moment, he imagined that he was flagging down one of the raiders' boats, but his first guess proved to be correct.

The launch was drifting in his direction. Nick swam furiously to intercept it, clambered aboard and sat dripping on the deck, congratulating himself for boarding it without risking a signal flare.

Exploring, he noticed an unexpected point of red against the dark planks. Stooping, he pulled out a shaft to reveal a jagged arrow head. Unlike the flimsy toys he'd made as a kid, this arrow was as thick as a Dult's finger – it had ripped through the decking like a shark's tooth through a wetsuit.

Nick approached the cabin. His fingers, wrinkled after their long soaking, tightened around the broken arrow. The cabin door was locked or blocked but it was simple enough to swing himself in through one of the smashed windows.

As he was winding some charge into the launch's dead radio, he heard a shuffling from under a tarp in the corner. Nick shuddered, he had a horror of rats, (not without reason, having lost a childhood friend to a virus carried by vermin).

Seizing a broken plank as a weapon, he moved towards the tarp. He had an instinct for which way a rat would run. As he made ready to strike, there was a stifled cry.

'I surrender!' called a frightened voice. Nick hauled the boy out from under the tarpaulin. He was no more than ten years old.

The kid, whose name was Jimmy, looked sick with fear but Nick was in a hurry.

Nick didn't want to ask, seeing the look in the boy's eyes, but he had to get on top of the situation.

'What happened Jimmy?'

'We was on the supply run to the Tower. When we got there, it seemed busy for a Monday...'

'Go on,' said Nick urgently.

'We came up behind this big old wooden boat. I dropped the anchor. "Busy for a Monday," I said to the Kaptain. The next thing I knew there were these tribal types swarming all over us. Horrible beggers in great big masks with...'

'Teeth?' interrupted Nick.

'Nets,' said Jimmy. 'They had nets.'

At that moment the radio crackled back into life.

'YPD units! Be advised: regroup at HMHQ immediately!

Backwards traveller

Jimmy's launch had been carrying ration packs to the prison.

'That's Rationpack C,' said the boy. 'We call it "The Cruel C." I wouldn't bother if I were you, it's not fit for a seagull.'

Nick needed the calories so he forced himself to eat it anyway. They'd been running for hours in the brewing storm, always taking the backwater routes and steering clear of the main channels.

'My sister's in the Catering Corps. She says they deliberately make up meals that taste like cat-sick and stuff, just for a laugh.'

Before Nick could reply, a familiar sight emerged through the mist.

Through his field glasses, Nick spotted two figures on the harbour wall, signalling frantically. The launch's radio was working but there was nothing being transmitted on the usual frequency, only a wailing drone like a hurdy-gurdy.

Nick dropped his ration pack in horror, two enemy vessels lay in wait on either side of the harbour entrance.

'Jimmy!' yelled Nick, 'Bring us about!'

'What?' said Jimmy open-mouthed, wishing the mist would dissolve the raider's ships as easily as it had made them appear. 'Nets!' he babbled.

'Quick Jimmy!' Nick pleaded, 'We're nearly in grappling range.'

When the kid didn't respond Nick seized him by the collar.

Dropping the petrified boy, Nick grabbed the controls. The launch came about too slowly for Nick's liking, their course was taking them straight across the bows of the first vessel.

They were close enough to see three ragged figures at the rail.

Without another word, Jimmy ran from the cabin. Nick went after him, but before he could prevent it, the kid had flung himself over the side, helmet, boots and all.

Nick found a life-preserver and threw it after the boy. As he considered what to do next, there was a metallic thwack and the deck in front of him exploded into a cloud of splinters.

Not waiting for the gunner's aim to improve, he weaved his way to the stern where a jetski was tethered. With a heave, the cable came loose and the ski floated free from its moorings. With relief, Nick saw that it was one of the new bio models with a kick-start. It fired on the first kick, and then came the best sound in the world: the stutter of a two-stroke engine.

To reach the gates of the inner harbour there was no choice but to run the gauntlet past the enemy flotilla.

When he wound back the throttle, the nose of the ski reared up and the bike accelerated, punching through the swells. As he raced alongside the raider's vessel he hardly had time to take in the sight of the nets.

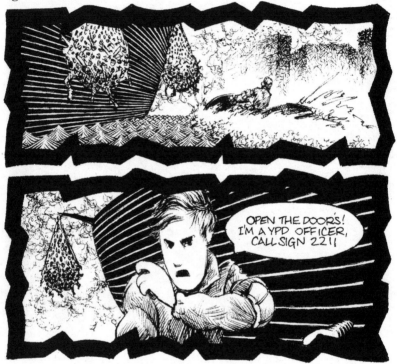

Clouds of arrows shot past him and fell hissing into the water.

It was like something out of medieval times, but with Nick on the jetski instead of a charger.

Crashing into a patch of bumpy water, Nick nearly lost control and he hung on with one hand as he fumbled with the radio, keying it frantically to try to warn the defenders of his arrival.

With an ear-splitting boom, a chunk of the harbour wall exploded and crashed into the water. The harbour gates were closing fast as the ski screamed through the narrowing gap.

Big stick

ON ONE SIDE OF THE HARBOR WALL THERE WERE MASKED RAIDERS WITH NETS, ON THE OTHER WAS A HUNGRY SERGEANT CALLED PHIL.

Nick had been cueing the radio on and off in a pattern of bursts, just like they'd taught him when he did his Comms training. Evidently the procedure had been lost on Phil.

'I thought you were another envoy,' explained the sergeant. 'The Mander's talking to the others now. Look, I don't suppose you've got any food have you? I'm famished. '

Nick gawped at the sergeant in disbelief, some personality types have trouble with empathy. However, at Hendon Marsh, talk of a lengthy siege had set everyone's stomachs rumbling.

In his ready room, the Mander was treating the APD envoys to a few lines he'd prepared to mark the occasion.

The YPD were in a different league, thought Mallard. It wasn't an overstatement to say that their leaders made his skin crawl. If the kids wanted their own police force, that was well and good, but why did they all have to dress up like clowns and give themselves titles like 'Supreme Master' or whatever?

Why was it always the mad ones who rose up the ranks like rats up a proverbial pipe? He didn't know who was worse, the lanky goon with the baton or the chilly little begger who was just about to pipe up now.

'So we're agreed then?' asked Haig. 'We'll negotiate.'

Chief Ohara hoped Mallard would play the game. It had been a risk taking him on a mission which called for this level of tact. The 'plain speaking,' that he set such great store in, could come over as bloody-mindedness.

Still, Mallard had dealt with the YPD before and managed not to start another age-war. It was worth the risk to have him in her corner, probably. So far, the DCI with the reputation for being outspoken had been unusually quiet. Mallard caught his boss's eye, making sure he had her attention.

THESE LADS ARE DAFT, IF THEY THINK THIS LOT WILL SET SAIL INTO THE SUNSET WHEN WE PAY THEM OFF.

WHAT OTHER CHOICE DO WE HAVE, APD?

The DCI let out a grim laugh.

'Well lad, as my grandad used to say, "sometimes tha needs to tek up a big stick",' said Mallard. 'And we'd better tek it up fast, or this lot'll be drifting back to us each month, like the scum on a bilge tide.'

'I'm afraid the Mander is right,' said Chief Ohara.

Mallard had expected as much, she was a decent boss, fairer than most but she was part of the 'talking' school of policing.

The corruption trials had changed the adult force, or 'police service' as they now had to call it once again.

'If they want a police 'service', send some beggin' waiters out on patrol,' was one of Mallard's favourite sayings.

In his view, the period of stability they'd achieved since the Climate Upgrade wasn't a given. Even now, they might be on the brink of a new Dark Age and such times called for warriors.

Haig ignored Mallard and addressed the demure Chief.

Mallard listened in amazement, this was madness, plain and simple. They were interrupted by the arrival of a messenger who tiptoed into the room, practically trembling as he approached. Mallard noticed it. How the YPD leaders treated their ranks set the tone for the whole organisation.

'We thought you ought to see this sir,' said the messenger. 'The enemy have sent out a boat.'

'Are we under attack?' asked the Mander, nearly dropping his baton.

'Negative, sir. It's a rowing boat. Intel reports indicate that there's only one man aboard.'

Mallard sighed. Why did they need 'reports' to tell them how many men were in a rowing boat?

'It looks like they want to negotiate,' said Chief Ohara.

'Is he armed?' asked Haig.

The messenger hesitated.

'No, not by the look of it sir...' his voice trailed off.

'What is it then?' demanded Haig.

'It would seem that he's carrying some kind of long wooden implement. They think it's a big stick of some sort.'

Geld talks

THE MAN STRODE INTO THE READY ROOM AND LOOMED OVER HAIG
LIKE A GIANT WHO'D BLUNDERED OUT OF THE PAGES OF A FAIRYTALE.

He was dressed in a most peculiar manner: leather boots and
belt; woollen waistcoat, and knotted kerchief. Although his clothes
were old fashioned in style, they were all clean and perfectly
pressed.

Mallard wasn't thinking about the stranger's clothing.

'What did he mean by 'long-friend?" muttered the DCI.

'Probably a term of greeting,' said Ohara, missing Mallard's meaning completely.

'When he says 'king', I expect he means 'leader' added the Mander, pleased with his observation.

Mallard let it go but eyed Haig suspiciously.

'Shall I speak first?' asked the Mander.

Ohara decided to show them that a woman's place wasn't by the fireside with the babies.

DO YOU SPEAK UNDER THE FLAG OF TRUCE?

BRING OUT YOUR KING! UNDER THE COWARD'S FLAG IF YOU LIKE. TIS SAID THAT THE SHARKS LIKE A WHITE WINDING SHEET FOR A TABLECLOTH.

'I wouldn't answer him if I were you,' said the Mander. 'In these cultures, tribal leaders sometimes fight each other in single combat.'

Mallard wondered which 'cultures' the Mander had in mind.

'I'm called Ohara. What is your name?' asked the APD Chief.

'Thorkeld,' answered the stranger, balling his broad fingers into a fist and hammering it down on the table.

The four officers reacted instinctively, jumping back.

'Come on yeildlings! I haven't got all day,' bellowed Thorkeld. 'Which one of you is the lord around here? It's not one of you little ninnies is it?' he cried, seizing Haig by the lapels of his coat and lifting him casually off the floor. 'In this weird-world 'tis said that the pups have the grey whiskers in the harness.'

'He might have a point there,' thought Mallard.

The giant let go and Haig dropped to the floor.

Thorkeld smiled. 'Geld talks eh? And there's the proof. That would be neat, wouldn't it? You'd pay up quick as a flash and send me down the whale road with a hold full of barrels?'

Thorkeld moved his gaze to each of them in turn.

Even the Mander, who prided himself on his speeches, didn't spot that the stranger's words had been rehearsed many times, in preparation for this moment.

'Yeildlings, there's a problem. The Stormfather has no need of your black geld.'

'We do not want war. Tell us what the Stormfather wants,' asked the Mander. 'We have other gifts.'

'You'd better have,' roared Thorkeld.

'Release the prisoners first,' said Ohara. 'They have done you no harm.'

'Never mind that,' said Haig. 'Listen to me. You can have whatever you like. Batteries? Food? Take whatever you need.'

Under my skin

THE MASKED FIGURE PUSHED A STICK INTO THE LITTLE GIRL'S ARM.

The girl stared up at the mask defiantly, and refused to move.

'My leg hurts!' she shrieked.

Jem stopped walking and turned slowly round to watch.

Without thinking, Jem stepped towards the masked figure and took hold of his wrist. Spinning on her heel, she lashed out with her boot and landed a powerful blow under the knee.

'Listen for the crunch,' her instructor had told her but Jem didn't hear anything. Grabbing the girl by the arm she tried to reassure her as they pushed past the interested bystanders.

'Do you like climbing,' she asked.

'Course I do,' answered the bewildered child. 'What kid doesn't like climbing?' thought Jem. Weaving through the throng of on-lookers, Jem led the child over to the mast.

'Reckon you can climb all the way to that little platform up there,' asked Jem pointing up. 'I'll be right behind you.'

'I dunno,' said the girl.

With a lot of encouragement the two of them struggled up the mast until they were high above the deck, looking down at the crowd. A tall young woman with coal-black hair appeared and beckoned to Jem, who looked for something to throw at her. A wooden bucket was the heaviest thing to hand.

Jem lowered the paintbrush, which was going to be her next missile and she eyed the female with suspicion.

'I'm Hafleur,' she said. 'Come down and the bone-setter will look at the young 'un's leg. You can follow me.'

'Why?' asked Jem slowly.

'We can't have you kicking my poor crew to pieces, can we?'

'Sorry,' said Jem. 'But they were scaring her.'

Jem looked down at the deck and considered the situation.

WHAT IF I DONT WANT TO GO?

YE CAN JOIN THE REST OF THE CATCH OVER THERE.

The masks were arranging their captives in lines. For every five masks there was one crew member, dressed in a similar style to Hafleur. 'Interesting look,' thought Jem.

The effect was historical – some wore pre-flood 'pirate' garb, whilst others wore tabards and tunics that looked like they belonged on a Viking.

Still, Hafleur kind of made her outfit work. At least she got to wear dangly jewellery, which certainly wouldn't be allowed in the YPD.

Jem suddenly remembered the bundle her mother had pressed into her hand, took it out and had a quick peek at it. It turned out to be a heavy three-pointed pendant on a chain that looked too flimsy to support the centre piece. 'Bizarre,' thought Jem. 'I can't imagine mother wearing this.'

Reluctantly, Jem had to accept Hafleur's invitation to join her on deck. Her six-year-old friend was in no state to mount an escape bid, so they decided to climb back down.

'Stand aside,' ordered Hafleur, clearing a path through the crowd.

As Jem followed Hafleur, she wondered what new kind of trouble she'd got herself into this time. Without warning, another mask stepped in, grabbed Jem by the wrist and pressed a metal stick into her arm. A momentary flicker of pain raced up the limb.

The sting soon dulled, but Jem could feel a foreign object floating under her skin.

'What in Lud's name have you done to me?' she demanded.

But no one was listening. Another masked figure had run over to Hafleur and the two of them were looking out over the water.

Following their gaze, Jem saw the shape of *The Billy Ruffian*.

Hafleur raised the glass to her eye in a practised sweep and then gave her orders to the masked figure.

One eight three

HAIG AND THE MANDER LOOKED DOWN AT THE MIXED-AGED CROWD THAT HAD GATHERED BEHIND THE INNER WALL OF THE HARBOUR.

Mallard was a bit surprised that the YPD had allowed so many 'Dults to take shelter alongside their children. The attack had really shaken things up.

The Mander and Ohara entered, fresh from the negotiations with Thorkeld.

'The final figure they want is 183,' he said.

'So we just tow them out and dump them there?' asked Mallard.

'I'm afraid that's about the size of it,' replied Ohara.

Thorkeld had only given them three hours to make the arrangements. The 'tribute' was to be delivered to a disused solar sub station nicknamed 'The Can' and then set adrift.

'And you agreed to that did you lad?' tutted Mallard.

'Thorkeld is a tough negotiator,' said the Mander, 'it could have been worse.'

'Oh well then, that's fine and dandy,' sighed Mallard.

'180 or so prisoners,' said Mallard cutting off the Head of Psyc
Ops. 'I reckon that's about all their fleet can carry.'

Mallard thrust his hands into his waistcoat pockets and scowled
like a bothered bear.

'I'll tell you something for nowt,' he said, 'there won't be 183
folk queuing up for Thorkeld's little pleasure cruise.'

'We've already anticipated that situation, obviously,' said the
Mander nervously.

'Obviously,' said Mallard.

'Haig has got a few officers from Psyc Ops out searching for
shirkers.'

'I bet he has.'

'Luckily the harbour is a secure area, so there's practically
nowhere to hide.'

'A most comforting thought,' said Mallard.

'Whether we like it or not DCI, lots must be drawn in order to
decide the 183 who will make up the tribute and it is our duty to

ensure that the draw is conducted in a free and fair manner.'

Sergeant Bates arrived, with a handful of straws and thrust them apologetically towards the Mander's assistant.

'Straws? Is this really the best you can do Bates?' asked the Mander turning to Chief Ohara to apologise. 'We would have liked to have organised a better system, with tickets, but I'm afraid there simply wasn't time to arrange it.'

Mallard cast a hawkish eye over Haig.

Reunion

As Jem was taken below decks, she noticed that the old ship was remarkably well put together. Harfleur ran a tight ship.

At last they came to a cabin, where a small group of captives were assembled. Then a voice called over to her.

'What are you doing here?' blurted Jem in amazement.

'Leading the assault on YPD HQ,' sneered Shami. 'Don't mind these bracelets, I'm just accessorizing for combat.'

'They got you too?' said Jem. 'That figures.'

Tribute

ON THE FLAGSHIP, THE CAPTAINS HAD GATHERED TO HEAR THE NEWS.

They had waited a long time for this. A murmur of excitement spread round the cabin and they all stood up as their bulky leader shambled into the room. Only a figure wearing a mask remained seated.

His mask was a piece of work indeed, it had no sharks' teeth, no horns or feathers, no intricate workmanship at all but it was somehow more fearsome for the lack of these things. A circle of spikes stood up from the neck like the rays of the sun. However roughly formed the 'Badmask' was, all eyes were drawn to it.

Harfleur shuddered. You could not stare at it without knowing that you were in the presence of something very old, and very bad indeed.

74

'Will it be enough?' asked a voice.

Badmask raised a hand in the air and a weird chant came from his crescent mouth.

Thorkeld spoke: 'We pray that 183 will be enough.'

'What did I tell you?' laughed the bearded man at his side. 'Soon The Stormfather will turn again!'

Badmask was still chanting: 'Turn, turn, turn!'

The rest of the group were sensible enough to give him a wide berth.

'Return to your ships,' ordered Thorkeld. 'We'll pick up the yieldlings and leave on the next tide.'

At the doorway, Thorkeld hailed the tall young woman with the raven hair.

'Harfleur my girl!' he called.

'Aye Thorkeld,' she answered with a smile.

'That little tub of yours is faster than *The Ruffian*, go ahead of us and prepare the Stormfather for our arrival.'

Final straw

Mallard exchanged a look with Ohara – they'd need to deal with this quickly if they were going to avoid a riot.

'I can assure you that both the YPD leaders and the APD will be drawing lots too,' called the Mander, winding more charge into the loud hailer.

'We weren't born yesterday son,' called the old man in the hat.

'Too piggin' right we weren't!' yelled another irate pensioner, doing a good job of making herself heard without amplification.

'Observers will ensure that the draw is fair,' called Ohara.

'Sir? Would you like to be a witness?' asked Mallard genially, as if he was officiating at an APD station boat raffle.

The pensioner was surprised to find himself being led up to the balcony, where the container of straws had just arrived.

Mallard held up his open palm to the aged observer and with a deep breath, he thrust his own hand deep into the box of straws.

When the DCI slid his chosen straw out, it was unmistakably long. Chief Ohara was next so she dipped her hand in and drew without comment or fuss.

The pensioner gasped and turned towards Mallard in shock, as if he'd condemned the woman herself.

'The draw was your idea I believe, Ma'am,' said Mallard. Taking the straw from Ohara's shaking hand, he swapped it for his own.

'No Mallard. I can't let you take my place, you've got family.'

'So have you Ma'am, younger than my Jem. Besides, someone's got to organise this lot in case Thorkeld's crew come back.'

In the crowd below, Nick waited for his turn. Phil, the hungry Sergeant was ahead of him, already dipping his chubby hand in.

'Get in there!' he cried, waving a long straw aloft like a trophy. As Phil let out a victory yell and joined the ranks of the saved, Nick stood gaping at the short straw he'd just drawn out.

Up on the balcony, Mallard walked past the smirking figure of Haig, half expecting a sarcastic quip. But the box of straws had now made its way around to the YPD leaders, so Mallard stopped to enjoy the show.

The Mander drew first, impressively calm as he reached into and slid out a straw. It was a long one.

Haig rapped his fingers on the lid of the box. Cursing the Mander for agreeing to this, he put his hand in and drew.

Cargo

'This Stormfather business… it ain't too pleasant,' said a pensioner, who'd spent most of the voyage worrying about the toilet facilities afforded by 'The Can.' Information never stays classified for long when the aged are about, thought Haig.

'I reckon this is it dear,' whispered the woman at the old man's side as she offering him a final sandwich. 'Let's pray it'll be brief.'

Haig prayed that the two wittering fools would await their fate in silence. That pair of idiots had jabbered enough last words between them to last ten lifetimes.

Mallard peered into the dark of the early dawn and mused…

A grey speck appeared on the horizon, and three minutes later it had turned into a T shaped dot, which then changed into a tiny ship gliding slowly towards them though the soft mist.

As the flagship loomed closer, some of the crowd started to cry, and began offering up prayers for deliverance.

Mallard was surprised to see that one old couple, bargers by the look of them, were actually rejoicing at the sight of the approaching ship.

'The Great Cargo! It's coming home, coming home!' they began to sing.

Nick hoped the bargers were right, and that all those little incense boats they'd spent their money on hadn't been burnt in vain. Was this the hallowed 'Ship of Dreams' coming for them, its hold crammed full of every possession they'd ever wished for?

Their song was so infectious that some of the others converted to the religion of The Great Cargo on the spot and joined in the dance.

But as the believers' boat came in, their shouts of joy turned to wails.

'Lud save us!' cried the portly woman.

Amidst the general panic, one figure was smiling.

'Well, well, well!' muttered Haig, saluting the masks at the rail.

Back at Hendon Marsh, the Mander was clutching a short straw in his gloved hand. He'd dreamed about this moment many times and now it had finally come to pass; but not by coups or plots – blind fortune had been his saviour.

In his mind, he wondered whether one hundred and eighty three lives was an acceptable price to pay? He had to conclude that it was cheap at half the price.

He decided to have the short straw framed and hung upon his ready room wall, for it was the lucky straw that had rid him of Haig. When the sergeant arrived, he quickly slipped the mask of grief back on.

Watch the stars

THE TWO MEN STOOD SHIVERING BENEATH A SHEET OF FAMILIAR
STARS.

'Are we on course?' asked Thorkeld, buttoning his coat against
the chilly night.

'Aye,' replied the helmsman. 'We'll steer west for the Bear's paw
until we're in line with the three stars of his paw, and then we'll
turn hard east for the Giant's eyes.'

Messages

By the steady roll of the deck, Nick guessed that they'd reached the open sea.

Every so often, another swell sent the ship pitching and its old timbers squeaked like piglets. Around Nick's ankle was a long iron chain like the ones he and Jem had discovered in the hold of the vessel the previous day. Now Nick understood why the hold had been empty – its cargo had not yet been taken aboard. Nick shuddered. He'd never been 'cargo' before.

One of the masks and a young woman in a hood were making their way down the slave deck's central gangway. Nick expected some new horror, but to his surprise he saw that the woman was dishing out medicine from a tube. The kid next to him stuck his hand out and got a measure of the pink ointment.

'Where do they think we're going to run to?' thought Nick rubbing the medicine into the wound on his arm.

The YPD used to use tracker chip implants, but these days they tagged offenders with pink collars, which had the advantage of making the criminals look like idiots. It was part of the thirty year drive to break the link between crime and glamour.

The prisoner in front dropped his food bowl and twisted around to pick it up. His moustache was unmistakable.

'Inspector Mallard!'

'Morning lad,' answered Mallard with a smile.

'I always promised myself a cruise, but this is ridiculous. Any news of that daft daughter of mine?'

Nick hesitated, wondering how much the DCI knew. The subject of what happened to Jem was a tricky one.

'She was captured,' said Nick. 'We were separated when...' Before he could finish, someone started causing a commotion.

'You're loco!' said the masked figure.

'Go to the one who wears the smiling mask. Tell him I'm here,' demanded Haig.

'Tell him yourself,' replied the mask, 'I'm not going anywhere near that one! He's bad medicine.'

'Is he really?' cooed Haig. 'Things have a habit of turning out better for people who do exactly what I say.'

'I'm not sure,' said Mallard, 'but when he first arrived, Thorkeld called Haig "long-friend."'

'Long-friend?' repeated Nick. 'What did he mean by that?'

'I reckon it means "old-friend" in their dialect,' said Mallard, '"yieldings" is what they call us, "the ones who give in".'

'Well they've got that right,' said Nick.

'Courage lad,' whispered Mallard. 'Our day may yet come. No heroics mind – we've got to find that daft daughter of mine. She was captured you say?'

'I'm afraid so,' muttered Nick, hesitating about how much detail to give out. 'There's one more thing, Jem might be with her mother.'

'Beggin' eck!' said Mallard. 'Give me Thorkeld's lot any day.'

Choker

Slipping down the edges of the ladder without touching the rungs, she strode off to make some final preparations.

Below decks, Jem waited patiently. Her sleep had been broken. She'd nodded off and found herself dreaming about ladders with legs, chasing human snakes around a board. She was thinking herself lucky that there'd been no masks in her dreams when one of them stepped in, carrying a stack of stolen ration packs and some bottled water. She recognised the mask immediately.

'Mother?' she whispered.

The masked figure placed the rations on the bench in front of her and remained completely still for a couple of seconds. Was it really her mother, or someone else in a similar mask? Before Jem could find out, the masked figure moved off down the corridor. Next, Jem felt something cold at her throat.

If the wooden bench hadn't been there, Shami's attack might have choked the breath out of Jem. Fortunately, it broke her fall partially, causing her attacker to lose hold for a moment.

'You're choking me!' spluttered Jem.

'That's the idea Officer.'

'Why?' coughed Jem, struggling to get her cuffed hands to protect her neck.

'Do you want the full inventory?' hissed Shami, re-establishing the choke hold. 'For my brother Asif. And for the others in your Tower, for the ones the YPD have disappeared. And for my friend the Fatman…'

Each name was punctuated with another wrench of the cuffs.

'They shouldn't have joined my mother's terrorists,' spluttered Jem.

'You don't deserve a mum like her,' thought Shami but she didn't say anything, preferring to let her hands do the talking.

With her attacker behind her, Jemima somehow got off her knees and pushed back, releasing the pressure on her neck. With a charge she bundled Shami back across the cabin into the wall.

Jem's hands were cuffed, but she raised them above her head and felt for the top of her assailant's scalp, cupping it carefully. Digging a finger into the pressure point under Shami's ear, she drew a wince. The hold on her throat eased and she grabbed Shami by the wrists – surprised at her opponent's wiry strength.

The next voice she heard belonged to Hafleur.

'Break it up!' she ordered, motioning to one of the masks to separate the pair. 'It's like this ladies, there's a piece of work to be done – but it ain't compulsory.'

'Good,' moaned Jem. 'Fraid I'm not up to it right now.'

Harfleur raised a finger to her lips.

'Ssssh! Quiet girl,' she ordered. 'I'm talking.'

'Sorry,' said Jem, but if it's anything dangerous, why not take old 'Chokey' over there? She's good with her hands.'

Shami scowled at Jem, and rattled her handcuffs.

'What happens if we say no?' she asked in a sullen tone.

'You haven't even heard about my task yet!' said Harfleur, her long dreadlocks swayed as she shook her head in disapproval.

'Okay,' said Shami. 'Go on.'

'I picked you two, because I reckoned you were up to the job. If your answer's nay, then I'll put you back with the yieldlings.'

'As you wish,' said Harfleur, beckoning them forward.

They trailed along behind Harfleur down series of tunnels, emerging at the foot of a wooden ladder that led to the deck above.

In the darkness, Jem lost her footing on the greasy rungs and Shami sniggered as Harfleur shot Jem a disappointed glance.

Up on deck there was a chemical smell to the air and shadows danced in the blazing tyre-light. Jem saw that they were now moored. As they disembarked, the jetty swayed beneath them.

Born on the water, Jem was often uncomfortable when she stepped onto land, but here she couldn't work out how she felt.

Harfleur lit a torch and told them to follow her. At first Jem thought she was walking up a pebbled track but she saw that it was paved with thousands and thousands of tiny pieces of plastic.

The winding path led them up past rows of square containers with doors and windows cut into their sides. The little tin houses creaked and groaned as they passed.

Smoke rose from their vents, but it wasn't the cheery smell of wood smoke, this was sour with a chemical tang to it. When Jem was about ten, her father had taken her to see the sink estates where bargers lived in semi-slum conditions not unlike this. 'Bone poor,' he'd called them.

'Who lives here?' asked Jem.

'That's my cousin's place,' said Harfleur pointing at a red container about three metres in length.

'Sweet box,' said Shami.

The jigsaw shantytown hugged the cliff, and the path that wound through it twisted back on itself a few times before finally bringing them out onto a open plateau.

On the way up the hill, Jem noticed a number of tall white poles with masks nailed to them. Now she stood before one, as it shuddered in the gusting wind.

'What is it?' she asked.

'A shrinemast,' said Harfleur, bowing her head. Inexplicably drawn, Jem went up to examine it.

'Don't touch it!' warned Harfleur. 'It means someone died there.'

Turn, turn, turn

About two hours later, the first of the 183 were trudging up the plastic track, past the row of shrinemasts.

It was nearly pitch dark but Mallard could read the phases of the night and by his reckoning, there were still a couple of hours to go before dawn. The wind had risen. Tattered strands that passed for hair were streaming from the masks on the white poles.

Nick sensed a presence far above him, as an eerie hum vibrated through the gloom.

The path climbed higher and higher, winding and snaking its way through the settlement until the ground began to flatten out.

The island was the shape of an upside down jelly. The steep sides where the huts clung to the cliff eventually gave way to a flatter area on the top, where the prisoners were huddling in groups.

As he climbed the last few steps, Nick wondered why the islanders chose to live in little containers dug into the cliff sides? It would be far easier to build houses here on the plateau where the ground was level. Then the wind bared its teeth and answered his question. The force of the gales would make life up here unbearable.

When Nick and Mallard finally crested the last rise, a line of guards in war-masks stood ready to greet them.

Nick suppressed a gasp. The masks were decorated with a jumble of plastic and bones: whiskers from seals; walrus tusks; feathers from herring gulls and teeth from Lud knows what. The sight of them made his skin crawl.

Mallard stuck his hand into his jacket pocket and pulled out a pen and a piece of paper.

'What are you doing?' whispered Nick, wondering how the DCI intended to get a message out from this forsaken place.

'Writing a Rivermail card for Chief Ohara and your Mander,' said Mallard. 'What shall we say? How about this:

Greetings from Thorkeld's Paradise Island. Wish you beggers were here, instead of us!'

Mallard tried to hand the card to a guard in a shark's-head mask but he wouldn't take it and it blew out of the DCI's grasp. The wind took it straight upwards.

'What do you make of the locals?' asked Nick as the guard waved his spear towards them.

'I think they're terrified,' whispered Mallard.

'Terrifying, more like,' said Nick.

An unexpected gust made the ground below their feet shake and thrum slowly like a bass string.

'I'm scared too,' said Mallard. 'But the question is: why do this lot need to put the frighteners on us?'

Nick didn't have an answer. Did there have to be a reason? That was one of Jem's favourite sayings.

A member of their welcoming committee stepped towards them with a flaming torch in his hand. Nick noticed that the guard's gloves were decorated like the fins of a deep-water fish.

'Nice morning for it Flipper!' laughed Mallard, offering the masked guard his hand. The man in the mask stepped back.

'When you think about it, we out number them by about four to one,' said Nick.

'Bang on!' said Mallard. 'And did you see the state of those shelters we just walked past? They were shocking.'

Nick nodded.

'Notice anything else?'

'The stench,' said Nick. 'I couldn't help noticing that.'

'Exactly,' said Mallard triumphantly. 'This lot are reduced to burning old bits of rubber for heat. I haven't spotted a scrap of wood anywhere in this place, save for their ships of course.'

'Lad,' said Mallard. 'These beggers are desperate. Perhaps we'll find out why, when we get to meet this Stormfather of theirs.'

'That's what I'm afraid of,' answered Nick.

It wasn't long before the masks had them on the move again.

Through the shadows Nick spotted the one known as Badmask. The mask he wore was perfectly smooth and bulbous, and its mouth hole was cut into a sweeping smile.

Nick didn't want to stare but his eyes were drawn to the pale monstrosity. He wondered about the artist who'd made that thing. What hand could have made a smile look so wicked?

Badmask had a troupe of little helpers, a gaggle of tiny masks who had gathered and stared leaping over a pile of burning tyres.

'Who are they?' asked Nick.

'Children, I think,' said Mallard. 'At least I hope it's kids, I don't think I could stand the sight of imps at this time in the morning.'

Unseen drummers begin to bash out a backbeat whilst the thrumming wind filled the hole where the bass would sit.

Nick turned to Mallard.

'Still reckon they're scared of us?' he asked.

Mallard nodded. 'It's a war-dance. To prove that they're strong, and that they're not afraid of us,' he answered.

The drum beat changed and the masks became more excited. One of them beckoned to Mallard, who tried to ignore him.

'For fill's sake!' cried Nick. "Do as he says Inspector.'

The Storm

From the top of the hill, Jem could see a bowl of light below her where hot sparks rose and shadows danced.

The pressure of the wind was almost unbearable and she and Shami were pinned back against a stone wall. Jem got the sense of something above her, a high tower disappearing up into the dark, whilst she felt the ground beneath her shaking in the eerie wind. A simple chant came rising from the bowl.

'Turn, turn, turn.'

Unknown to Jem, far below, her father was leaping around a pile of burning tyres with a broad grin on his face.

'I never fancied myself as much of a dancer,' he puffed. 'Mind you, it's amazing how fast you can move when Flipper over there digs his spear in your ribs.'

'Whatever they've got planned, I wish they'd get on with it,' sighed Nick.

Badmask led the others in a frenzied dance.

'Hang about,' said Mallard. 'Looks like the fun's starting.'

'It won't be long now,' said Nick. 'I'll bet that this Stormfather of theirs is going to show up at the crack of dawn.'

'Bloomin' exercise!' wheezed Mallard. 'I don't think I can last out till then.'

'Dance on the spot for a bit and save your energy,' suggested Nick.

'Is there anything in that precious YPD manual of yours for times like this?'

'Fraid not,' said Nick. 'We could try to distract them and escape. But then what? Steal a boat?'

Mallard didn't answer. He'd stopped dancing and was pointing up the hill. The moon had shaken off its cloudy shroud.

The drums fell silent and the masked dancers cast themselves down onto the ground. Mallard let out a wild, hysterical laugh.

'What's so funny?' snapped Nick.

'The Stormfather! He's not a man. He's a wind turbine!'

In the moonlight there stood a tall column, and on top of it was an unmistakable three-bladed shape.

'You don't think...' began Nick.

'I'm afraid so,' grunted Mallard. 'We're being sacrificed! To a bloomin' windmill.'

Tribute

Jem gasped as she asked Harfleur the question.

'Take this rope and secure it to the blades,' said Harfleur.

'How in Lud's name do we get up there?' asked Jem.

Harfleur pointed to a metal ladder which was set into the base of the tower.

'That's it?' asked Shami, searching Harfleur's eyes for a catch.

'That's it,' said Harfleur throwing her a rope. 'But it ain't so simple – you'll need to cling on like limpets or they'll be raising shrinemasts for the pair of you.'

'So why not do it yourself?' asked Shami.

'I'm not allowed, we can't let them see us disrespecting it.'

Jem stood gaping at the messenger, she was sure she recognised his round face from somewhere but she couldn't place him.

'I must go,' said Harfleur handing them each a wind up torch. The torches were YPD issue by the look of them, with red filters over their lenses. 'Flash me a signal to let me know when you've attached your ropes to the blades.'

Jem nodded, still staring at the boy.

'Climb safe!' called Harfleur, taking the other end of their ropes and uncoiling them carefully behind her as she went. 'One more thing. Whatever happens, do not follow me down the hill.'

'Hey! Your name's Saul isn't it?' called Jem to the boy. 'You were imprisoned in the Bloody Tower. How did you get here?'

'E.R.S. scheme,' he yelled through the wind. 'Not that I'd have taken an 'early' if I knew I'd end up on this stinking fill heap.'

With Saul's puzzling words still running round her brain, Jem looped the rope around her waist and turned to the ladder.

For reasons she couldn't fathom, Jemima found the thought of ladders far more terrifying than the idea of scrambling up a rock face, or scaling a remote cliff. Their smoothness and apparent simplicity sent her nerves jangling. She tried to imagine herself standing safely at the top; but the image changed and she saw herself clinging desperately, her grip weakening, whilst the old familiar panic welled up inside. What would it feel like to freeze mid-climb, knowing that however hard you willed your hands to move, the puppets would refuse their master's bidding. Even more puzzling was the possibility that she might actually want to let go, give herself to the wind and fly like a hayseed.

The ladder was absurdly long and the climb was as challenging as Harfleur had warned. Triumphantly giddy, Jem hauled herself onto the platform half-way up and sat gasping in the searing wind.

'It's been good knowing you lad,' said Mallard, in a low voice.

Badmask

A TALL GIRL IN A WHITE MASK LED HAIG THROUGH THE
CROWD OF DANCERS.

'You want to meet the man in the smiling mask,' she said
hurriedly. 'Well there he is, dancing around that fire.'

Haig was used to getting others to do what he wanted, so it
never even occurred to him to thank her.

'Good luck to you!' she called, making a hurried departure
through the throng.

The one called Badmask spotted Haig and stopped dancing.

Dead point

JEM WOULD HAVE HAPPILY LEFT THE FINAL LEG OF THE CLIMB TILL DOOMSDAY.

However, Shami was already coming up the ladder behind her, so Jem embarked on the final stage.

A second ladder, thinner than the first, led up to the turbine's central pivot, which looked like the propeller of an ancient plane. Jem climbed up to the pivot, tied on a safety rope and began the dangerous traverse along the blade to attach her line.

The best way to climb onto the blade itself was to reach a grab handle set into a recess on its face. With an explosive spring, she leapt across and up, waiting for the 'dead point' where her upwards momentum and gravity cancelled each other out. Stretching, she grabbed for the handle, but a freak gust swept her off the sail, leaving her dangling helplessly from the safety line.

'Please!' cried Jem, hating herself for begging. She could only watch as Shami climbed out and secured her rope to the tip of the opposite blade before disappearing down the ladder.

Only the thin safety line prevented Jem from a fatal fall. But if she could build enough momentum, she might be able to swing herself back over to the ladder and catch hold of a rung.

She swung as hard as she could. The rope moved and she began to sway towards the ladder but the tearing wind was constantly working against her. After three more tries, it was clear that she'd never be able to generate enough speed to reach it.

Craning her neck back, she peered upwards and considered the alternatives. Climbing back up her own rope seemed crazy, but it was a trick that Nick had taught her in training.

Unhooking herself was the scariest part – now she really knew how it felt to take your life in your hands. Grip was the key to climbing, Nick had said. Gripping too hard would sap your energy, (until your forearms gave out). But if you didn't grip hard enough... Well, the results of that were obvious.

Once unclipped, she took the rope between her legs, around her calf and back past the instep of her boot. This last twist formed a brake to stop herself slipping downwards.

Gasping, she began to climb, pulling up with her arms before twisting the rope around her foot to pause for a few breaths. In this way she hauled herself back up her own rope, inchworm style, until she reached the ladder and clambered back onto it.

Jem didn't fancy risking the wind's relentless power again. She was about to turn back when she spotted something on the edge of the sail. It was a little groove, just small enough to offer a toe-hold for her boot tips. Using this for purchase, she inched out along the blade. At last, the end came into sight and she secured her rope to the anchor point at the tip of the blade. Her line fastened, Jem edged slowly back to the safety of the central ladder.

White cross

Far below, Harfleur saw the signal she'd been waiting for: two red lights flickering like planets in the night sky.

They'd already assembled the prisoners into a couple of working parties. But before they began their task, Thorkeld addressed the crowd.

TO MAKE THE STORMFATHER TURN WE MUST ALL HAUL TOGETHER.

THANK THE SEVEN BLOOMIN' SIRENS FOR THAT! FOR A MOMENT. I THOUGHT...

'I know,' said Nick, who was standing at his side. 'I thought we were...'

'What ever gave you that idea?' interrupted Mallard. 'Not the old ropes and drums routine? But what's Thorkeld planning now, I wonder?'

'If he wants to get the wind turbine going, I don't rate his chances,' said Nick. 'The mechanism must be ninety years old if it's a day. It'll be rusted solid.'

'Never underestimate the power of slave labour,' said Mallard. 'When that old Viking gives the signal, pull for your begging life!'

As the workers took hold of the ropes, the drummers struck up again, this time with a steady boom.

The cable went taut and the people gasped and heaved as the drums urged them on. Nick looked up at the turbine's sails, and for a brief moment he thought he could see them shifting ever so slightly.

'It's moving!' cried Harfleur.

'Come on!' bellowed Thorkeld. 'Haul now!'

The teams gave another great heave. Bent-legged, they braced against the strain and pulled their hearts out. Nick's palms burned as the rope tore into them.

In this way, they sweated at the ropes until the moon was setting in the western sky, but still the blades wouldn't budge.

Haig stood near Badmask watching. When the work gangs lay exhausted and gasping, he walked up to him and looked the pale menace straight in the sockets where its eyes should have been.

Badmask whispered to a cloaked figure at his side and the translator approached nervously. Others wanted to run from the sight of this mask, but Haig seemed unaffected by its hollow glare

'He wants to know how to make it turn,' he said in a trembling voice. 'I knew this would happen. You'd better answer him quick.'

Haig paused, processing the translator's squirms. He simply could not understand how one person might be frightened senseless on another's behalf.

The translator eyed Haig in disbelief. Haig strode towards Badmask and pointed up at the wind turbine which stood brooding under the murky clouds. He alone truly understood why they worshipped this wind-devil. He let out a brittle laugh.

'Tell Badmask he already knows the answer,' he said.

'The Stormfather will never turn without blood,' said Haig.
'You know I'm right! Go on! Tie an offering to the blades!'

The translator talked with Badmask whilst Haig waited for an
answer. At last the cloaked man walked back over to report.

'What did he say?' asked Haig, in agitation.

'He wants to know who's first?' came the answer.

Haig seemed surprised by this and scratched his chin.

'I don't know,' he said. 'Whoever will please the Stormfather.'

But before his translator could pass on the message, Haig
shouted at him to stop, pushed through the crowd and snatched a
small wooden pot out of a mask-maker's hand.

'Tell him I will choose the tribute,' called Haig as he pushed through the throng, aiming his paintbrush at possible candidates. A few moments later, he stood before Thorkeld.

'Now we'll see who's the Yieldling,' he laughed.

Thorkeld towered above his accuser, and it seemed likely that the giant would reach out with one of his great arms and swat Haig like a mosquito. But instead, Thorkeld stood transfixed.

'Look at him!' cried Haig, pointing the brush accusingly. 'He cannot make it turn! He will never make it turn!'

Then the crowd began to chant: 'Turn, turn, turn.'

Haig dipped the brush into the bucket and strode towards Thorkeld. When he was sure that everyone was watching, he slashed a white cross over the big man's face. Thorkeld flinched.

'Now he's ready!' laughed Haig. 'But who's next?'

Badmask's followers roared their approval and began to dance again. Haig joined in for a few jerking steps but he thought better of it when he spotted another familiar face in the crowd.

Nick looked at Mallard, who was standing next to him. The white paint was running down his face but his tie and waistcoat were still remarkably dapper. The other workers backed away from the paintbrush in a panic; Haig had turned it into a weapon.

Nodding at Mallard, Nick slowly unbuttoned his YPD armband and cast it on the ground. It slipped into a muddy puddle.

'Hey! Head of Brush Ops,' called Mallard. 'There's a new slogan for you!'

"People Matter!" It's got a ring to it, you never know, it might catch on one day.'

'A day you'll never see,' cried Haig, 'but hang around for it.'

As Badmask's followers charged towards Mallard, tears of frustration ran down his paint-spattered face. This mob would surely fall on him and Nick, and cast them off the cliffs onto the teeth of white rocks. But a command stopped them in their tracks.

Upside down

Nick struggled, but the ropes held him fast.

'Count your blessings,' called Mallard. 'It could be worse!'

'Could it really?' yelled Nick. 'How exactly do you work that out?'

'Two shakes of a lamb's tail ago, that lot were about to give us a closer view of their fine white rock formations. But now we've got our long-friend Thorkeld here to entertain us with his charming tales of the olden days.'

'I don't yarn with Yieldlings,' called Thorkeld.

'Thorkeld, you old smoothie,' laughed Mallard. 'I suggest you give up all of this ancient mumbo jumbo and start making sense.'

Mallard, 'How come this blade that we're tied to has been repaired recently?'

Thorkeld stayed as silent as a burial mound.

'Nice job,' said Mallard. 'Very neat. Which Viking managed that? Erik Blowtorch? Or his mate Sven the Spotwelder? Come on man! What do you think Haig has planned for your friends when the Stormfather still won't turn after we're all dead and gone?'

'It is a long tale,' called Thorkeld. 'I fear it will do no great good, but I suppose you might as well hear it. I was the lead researcher on a scientific survey vessel. Storm force winds blew us here by chance. Our ship was lost and there were only a handful of survivors including our doctor and the lead engineer, nicknamed Fatman.'

'Did he say Fatman?' yelled Nick from the opposite blade.

'Yes. Go on Thorkeld,' said Mallard.

'What these people call an 'island' is in fact the heart of a chain of floating factories for generating electricity from the wind.'

'How they first came upon their 'island', I cannot tell. They do not remember themselves, and they have no written history. But it is likely they've lived here since around the time of what we call 'the event', when their old world was washed away, like ours was.'

'Over time, they began to worship the wind turbine – and their priests would hang 'offerings' from its great blades.'

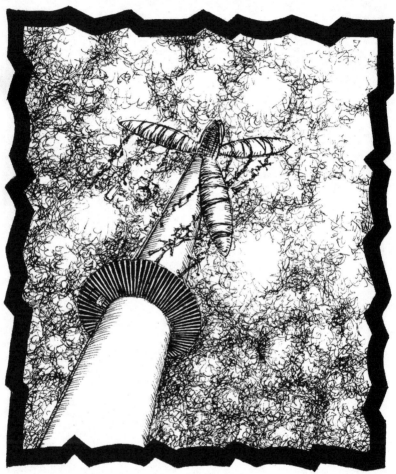

'Life here was a constant struggle. Storms tore away their shelters in the winter and freak waves came after the summer lull, taking many lives. Every family has its shrinemast to bear witness.

The tribe was as surprised as us when we arrived. We handed

out trinkets to try to make friends – the Fatman gave out cards from his tarot deck.

At first we were tolerated, but when the seas went flat for a month, ill fortune took hold. One priest was at the root of their hostility, we called him 'Badmask'. At the time we couldn't understand, but I worked out what must have been said later...'

'Alas, they did not listen to the wise women. They scraped our skin clean and decked us with seaweed garlands, then Badmask's followers marched us up here and tied us to the blades. Not one of us thought we'd last the night, but then a miracle happened: a hundred-year storm blew in. The seas were so high that the spray wet my beard. But the force of the gale made the blades of the turbine turn around, by one notch…'

'They cut the Fatman down first and he seized his chance. He showed them a card from the tarot deck – the hanged man – and then pointed at me, hanging from the sail by my foot. The tribe didn't need much convincing after that. They all sank to the ground, moaning and babbling and blaming Badmask for what had happened. Before we could stop it, they cast him away.'

'What? You mean they set him adrift in a boat?' yelled Nick.

'No… they cast him to the seaghasts on the white rocks.'

'If Badmask is dead, who's that dancing round the bonfire?'

'Badmask came back. Masks are very important to these people. They have a funny habit of outliving their owners.'

'The tribe worshiped us like gods. Fatman was the Head god.'

'Lucky her!' Nick observed.

'It was only symbolic,' said Thorkeld. 'She was against it.'

'I bet she was!' said Mallard.

'The Fatman promised them that we'd make their Stormfather turn, so we set to work.'

'There were two problems,' continued Thorkeld. 'First-ly, we needed manpower – to make the blades turn. There were few people in the tribe. Some were fast learners, like Harfleur but most were too frightened to touch their god. The other issue was technical, there was a part we needed; a powerful magnet. When we opened the control panel it was missing, but it is unlikely that the tribe could have taken it...'

Before Thorkeld could finish the tale, Nick let out a scream. Something whizzed past his face and bounced off the sail with a rattle. The rattle turned into a clatter and soon the air was thick with missiles.

As suddenly as it had started, the attack ceased.

Not daring to respond to the voices from below, the three prisoners now hung quietly, and the minutes dragged.

The only sounds to be heard above the ceaseless wind stream were the cries of the gulls circling the white rocks.

Nick let out a sigh. Then he heard a croak of stifled laughter coming from Mallard's side of the turbine.

'What's up over there?' called Nick, as loud as he dared.

'Sorry lad,' sniggered Mallard.

'What's so funny?' asked Nick.

'I think I just found out how the white rocks got their name.'

'How?' asked Nick, in a whisper.

'Only the seagulls have the answer,' called Mallard, 'and one of them just left a big helping of it on Thorkeld's beard.'

Nick began to shake uncontrollably with laughter, and he almost missed a familiar voice calling from above.

'Nick!' it hissed. 'Nick! Are you OK?'

'I thought I was, till I started hearing voices.'

'It's me!' said the voice. 'I'm climbing down to you. Hang on!'

'Not a problem,' said Nick. 'But then what?'

'I dunno, I'll untie you or something,' said Jem.

'Great!' said Nick. 'What about the others?'

'Sorry! Fraid I haven't planned that far in advance. Here I come!'

'Er Jem, there's something important I need to tell you...' called Nick.

But before he could get the rest of his sentence out, Jem was already lowering herself down on a line.

'I know, thanks for saving you from being sacrificed. Well don't ever forget...'

At that moment, Jem heard the last voice she expected to hear: it was the voice of her own father, bellowing like a bull horn.

Procession

HAIG INSPECTED HIS GANG OF NEW RECRUITS WITHOUT ENTHUSIASM.

The 'White-tips' uniform was a bit of a mish-mash; part YPD and part 'tribal'. They were mainly distinguishable by the fact that each soldier in the new force carried a spear with a white tip.

White was the obvious symbol for Haig to pick: the colour of purity and youth would tie in nicely with the tribe's sacred 'white rocks'.

It was a pity that they couldn't follow orders.

'Out with him I say!' shrieked Haig.

Even having the power of life or death, couldn't save him from having to work with incompetents.

'Sorry,' muttered a newly appointed Sergeant.

'You will address me as "Sir," at all times,' reminded Haig.

The Sergeant gave a sign to the White-tips and the reject was cast out with a boot in the face for his trouble. Haig's deputy began to wonder about his recent promotion.

'What time is it?' asked Haig.

'Nearly dawn Sir!'

'"Nearly" dawn is not a time,' corrected Haig.

'Sorry sir! But we're lighting the torches just like you said.'

Cries and whispers

'JEMIMA LOVE, YOU'VE REALLY GOT TO LEARN TO LISTEN,' CRIED MALLARD, SHAKING HIS HEAD.

Jem wrenched at the ropes but that didn't work so she tried picking at them. That was no good either – she was entangled.

'Thanks for trying to rescue us,' called her father.

'You're welcome!' sighed Jem, pulling frantically at the lines.

'Next time, think it through love, and get it done properly!'

'Twist it to the left,' called Nick. 'Is there any more slack?'

'It's no good. I'm roped up tighter than a barger's swan.'

Jem stopped struggling and looked in Nick's direction.

'Come on then, when did you start hanging out with my dad?'

Nick explained their story, and some of Thorkeld's too. As he came to the part about the Fatman, Jem noticed Nick's mood dip.

'Orders!' called Mallard. 'Fraid we've all had to follow 'em.'

'I hate to admit it, but dad's right,' said Jem. 'You were...'

'Only following orders?' suggested Nick. 'Just like all of those masks down there are following theirs.'

White bands of quartz in the granite sky signaled the approaching dawn whilst distant storms flung lightening at the sea.

'Thorkeld?' called Mallard. 'Scratch an itch for me. Why did you choose to carry on like Vikings and pirates?'

'It wasn't about being Norsemen or buccaneers; we just wanted to create a warrior culture that the tribe would understand.'

'Something's bothering me too,' said Jem. 'I met this kid called Saul earlier. He was dressed like one of the tribe but I recognised him from ages ago, back in the Bloody Tower.'

'Was he captured when our long-friend here attacked?' asked Nick

'No!' said Jem. 'He said he'd been sent here on early release.'

'Early release?' thundered Mallard. 'Thorkeld?!'

'Our Mander said: There's room enough in the Tower for every young person who defies the law!' said Nick. 'And he was right! Because Haig was letting them out the back door and dumping them out here,'

'Only not enough of them it seems,' said Mallard.

'We needed more manpower, to get the Stormfather turning,' explained Thorkeld. But whatever he said next was lost as the wind switched direction and began to race over from the west.

'I reckoned Haig was up to something,' called Mallard. 'From the first time we met.'

'Well, they ought to know,' said Nick. 'They're not exactly all sweetness and light themselves.'

The buffeting wind dropped for a moment.

'That's unfair,' said Thorkeld. 'The tribe have a fascinating culture. I'm afraid you've only seen one side of it.'

'I've got a horrible feeling we're about to see more of that side of it!' said Jem pointing down at a fan of lights that had appeared on the hillside below.

One of the little lights burst out of the circle and began racing towards the base of the Stormfather at full pelt.

'Look!' said Nick. 'I think they're about to start the ceremony.'

'Oh no!' moaned Mallard.

'What's wrong?' asked Nick.

'That means the drum workshop is going to start again in a moment. My head's killing me.'

Jem, who had been unusually quiet, turned to Thorkeld.

'Only Harfleur and a few of the others are brave enough,' said Thorkeld.

Three points of light peeled off in pursuit of the first, but before it got to the base of the platform, the pursuers halted and the lone torch ran on until it passed out of sight.

Second coming

THE SUDDEN COMMOTION MADE HAIG TURN HIS ATTENTION FROM THE NEW MASK THAT HE'D ORDERED FOR HIMSELF.

Springing up, he saw the absurd sight of three of his 'White tips' careering up the hill towards the Stormfather.

'What is going on?' he enquired. 'Explain!'

Haig's deputy scrambled to his feet so fast that he slipped on the wet ground and fell, before jumping up enthusiastically again.

'It's an intruder Sir!' he yelled. 'I'll get on it, this second.'

My generation

A FEW MINUTES LATER, JEM HEARD NOISES COMING FROM THE GANTRY, AND SOON A FAMILIAR FACE SWUNG INTO VIEW.

'Break out the best china,' cried Mallard. 'We'll have a family reunion 30 metres up.'

'Charmed to see you too,' said River, securing her line to Jem. Unlike her daughter, she had planned ahead and brought extra ropes and climbing harnesses. She also had an impressively large knife with a blackened blade, which she now waved playfully at her ex-husband.

'Quickly Jem, we're leaving,' she said. 'We'll be abseiling down, so do remember to use your feet to push off the base of the tower as we descend.'

Jem fixed River with her best stare.

'Mother! I'm not leaving without the others,' she said.

'Alright, you can bring Policeboy over there,' said River, 'as long as there's a unit on climbing in his manual.'

'In fact there are two relevant units,' thought Nick, 'one on ropes and the other on spans.' Luckily, he didn't mention this.

River's knife was passed along to him and soon he'd cut himself free and was clinging on for dear life.

'Looks like I'm doing the school run this morning,' said River, throwing him a line and harness. 'Come on you two.'

'Mother!' snapped Jem. 'We can't leave anyone behind.'

'Bring your father too?' laughed River. 'Can't we dump that Yorkshire pudding?'

'Fraid not. He's a bit borderline sometimes, but he's a keeper.'

'Speak for yourself. Come to think of it, there's one 'borderline' friend that I need to find too.'

'Throw me the spare ropes,' called Nick. 'I'll traverse over and free the others.'

It was no surprise to Jem that Nick made such fast work out of this tricky manoeuvre, even in the vicious wind.

With a level of climbing skill which she found rather annoying, he scaled the blade to the central pivot in a flash. Once safely at the ladder, he secured the lines and scrambled down the opposite blade towards the other two.

He reached Thorkeld first, cut him loose and helped the big man to the safety of the steel ladder.

By the time Nick had gone back and released Mallard, the other three in the party had made it down to the gantry.

As Nick climbed down to meet them, a sudden hail of missiles shrieked through the air, bouncing off the turbine's blades. Nick arrived on the gantry to find that Haig's new force was half way up the lower ladder and nearly upon them.

The masked climber crashed back down the ladder but the on-slaught from below continued. A spear crashed towards River's ear, but Mallard stuck out a hand and caught it by the shaft.

'There you go dear,' said the DCI, handing it to her, stick end first. 'Here's another one for you to beat me with. It's a good long 'un too.'

River smiled sweetly at him and joined Nick in the fray, hurling anything she could find down the ladder at their attackers. Another mask fell with a cry, but below stood many more, waiting to take his place.

Arrows pinged onto the gantry floor like hailstones, but weirdly none seemed to be getting anywhere near their mark.

'Hey Jemima love! It's a good job those archers down there haven't been on any of your training courses,' remarked Mallard.

'Just wait till Haig gets started with them,' said Jem.

Then she realised her father had a point. At the rate that they were being fired at, they should be stuck like porcupines by now.

'How come they can't hit us?' she asked.

'Pressure imbalances caused by the blades of the turbine,' said Thorkeld, prising away at a panel in the centre of the Stormfather. 'No arrow can fly straight through turbulence like that.'

Something loud smacked into the central column, taking a wisp of Jem's hair with it.

'Looks like spears can fly through it,' said Nick.

Thorkeld turned to River.

'Doctor River,' he asked formally but sternly. 'Do you happen to have our magnet in your possession?'

Thorkeld fixed her with an accusing stare.

'And failing that, do you happen to have any tea and crumpets?' asked Jem, offering him one of the spears she'd just collected. 'They're actually coming, as I've been pointing out.'

'She's right! Can we all get throwing!' yelled Nick, planting a boot in the chest of an attacker who'd made it up the ladder.

'I don't have your magnet,' snapped River.

'Don't believe her,' sighed Thorkeld. 'She and Fatman wanted the magnet for themselves. They told me some nonsense about a secret organisation they were forming.'

'Have you suddenly grown a conscience Thorkeld?' hissed River. 'You attacked and abducted 183 people remember?'

'We needed manpower to start the Stormfather. You know very well that the tribe won't touch it,' he replied.

'Why did you steal it?' asked Jem, turning to her mother with wide-eyes.

Two spears suddenly arrived in quick succession, it seemed as if the attackers were finally finding their range.

'Please…' began Thorkeld.

'Save your breath Fishbeard,' River snapped back at him. 'I don't have it. Search me if you don't believe me.'

Her eyes swelling with tears, Jem reached into an inner pocket and pulled out the little bag that her mother had given her before.

'Jemima! Don't!' cried River, making a grab for Jem's hand. Jem snatched it away and revealed the unusual 'necklace'.

'How did you know?' gasped River.

Jem felt herself shrivel inside; in her hand she held the only thing her mother had ever given her, and now she found it wasn't a proper present. It was a lever, not a gift.

'You've got strange taste in jewellery mum, but this is a bit weird, even for you,' said Jem as she handed it over to Thorkeld.

Thorkeld flipped open an inner panel revealing a fluorescent green logo which read 'Storm-farmer type II.'

'Look! The Stormfather is a Storm-farmer!' cried Nick. 'It's the name of the manufacturer of the wind turbine.'

'Yeah, yeah – we get it!' said Jem, tears welling in her eyes.

Thorkeld pushed hard and the magnet clicked into place.

'Er, is this wise? Starting this thing up while we're...?' began Mallard, then he stopped in mid-sentence.

The machine began to hum and then buzz. The platform trembled as the static-charged air made Jem's hair stand on end.

The group stood staring at the blades – they shook and juddered – but still they would not turn.

'The sails are now highly charged!' warned Thorkeld.

The Masks stopped attacking and far below, the crowd fell to the ground. Haig's White-tips stayed on their feet, but watched transfixed as the sparks rippled and coiled down the sails.

'Not turning then?' said River. 'Can I have my magnet back?'

'It's seized,' said Thorkeld. 'It can't generate till the sails turn.'

'You lot are always talking about 'manning' things. It's as if we girls don't have arms.'

'Well said Jemima!' called River. 'All that Viking role play has turned them into hammer-brains.'

'All right ladies you've made your point,' groaned Mallard. 'You can 'girl' the ropes, if you prefer. Just climb down fast before they start attacking again.'

'Wait!' said Nick. 'You need to get it turning right? I'll climb up and re-attach the lines. It won't do any turning without that.'

'Good lad!' said Mallard. 'At least one of us men has still got an operational brain.'

As Nick climbed back up to tie on the ropes, Jem was first down the ladder, followed by River, with Thorkeld and Mallard, who were the slowest climbers, bringing up the rear.

'Ready!' called Nick from the gantry.

As Thorkeld reached the base of the ladder, Badmask's followers and Haig's White-tips stood gaping at the electric light show.

Spotting Harfleur by a blazing tyre, Thorkeld ran over to her.

'Help me 'Fleur, we've got to try the ropes again! It will turn now, I'm sure of it!'

Harfleur looked at Haig and Badmask, then finally back to Thorkeld. Nodding to him, she stepped calmly towards the ropes.

'Don't touch!' hissed Haig. Despite the flicker and buzz of the electric show, he still commanded the crowd.

Haig trotted over and borrowed a spear from one of his White-tips.

'Whoever touches those ropes is a dead man,' he said.

'There they go again,' said Jem. 'Did you hear that? A dead 'man'

Hafleur joined Jem on the rope.

'Girls can die too, you know!' said Jem.

Haig drew his arm back in a flash and raised the spear.

Jem gasped as Harfleur side-stepped the spear. She was just thinking up a cutting remark to fling at Haig when she heard a horrible thud, followed by a wail.

Thorkeld, who'd been securing the ropes, lay writhing in agony.

Harfleur screamed in anguish, louder than the wounded man.

'Thorkeld! Thorkeld! I'm sorry!'

'Get them on the ropes,' moaned the fallen giant. 'Get it turning Fleur.'

As River rushed to help him, Haig strode over to Badmask and his cabal of masked followers.

'Observe! Here I stand, within the scared circle, and I have not been cursed or struck down. In fact, The Haigfather, as we shall be calling him, is very pleased to see me.'

He pointed his paintbrush at the crackling structure above him.

'Just look at him. He's practically glowing with pleasure!'

Badmask's followers began to waver. Some of them stepped over to Haig's crew and the others stayed and looked to their leader.

Haig lunged at Badmask with the paintbrush.

As trails of white paint dripped down the mask, Harfleur called to the crowd of onlookers.

'Never mind those two, we've got to get the Stormfather turning. To the ropes!'

Jem and Harfleur were joined by a good few of the tribe.

The Stormfather held no more fear for them, its god-like reign had come to an end.

Mallard and Nick joined Jem at the ropes, and soon a sizeable work party was ready to give it another try.

'Haul!' cried Harfleur. 'Haul away now!'

Slowly at first but then faster and faster, the great sails began to rock; and then to shake; and at last they started to rotate on their own as the cheers of the crowd rose upwards on the wind.

The island erupted with cries of celebration as the blades picked up speed and began to spin freely.

Badmask shuffled towards Haig, paying no attention to the Stormfather. Nobody noticed him as he closed in on his rival, they were still too busy celebrating.

'Watch it!' warned Nick, seizing Jem by the arm and pulling her towards him. A rope had become caught on one of the sails and was thrashing about wildly, as if whipped by an invisible hand.

Meanwhile, Haig was proving a handful for Badmask. The masked man aimed blow after blow; but whether he punched or kicked, the slippery little runt always seemed to evade him. Puffing and panting, Badmask took a cord out of his pocket, enjoying the squeal of leather as he drew it tight between gloved hands. Seeing his purpose, Haig sprang towards him, tearing wildly at the mask and screaming at him to show his face.

As they wrestled, the pair rolled nearer and nearer to the base of the turbine and Haig became tangled in the flailing guide rope.

'Help me!' he screamed, clinging desperately to his opponent and trying to use him as a shield. For a brief moment, the great sails stuttered and began to slow.

But it was too late for either the man or the youth to free himself. Inertia gathered and the next rotation jerked the pair of them up through the mechanism before spitting them high into the air.

Free of its burden, the Storm-farmer started to spin faster.

Suddenly the crowd began to murmur, then they cheered wildly.

'Look at the lights!' cried Jem.

Way out into the ocean as far as the eye could see, a string of illuminations appeared as a chain of wind farms flickered into life.

Meanwhile, as Harfleur gaped in amazement at the motionless body of her fallen friend, Mallard turned to River.

'This was Thorkeld's dream,' sobbed Harfleur, pointing at the row of twinkling lights. 'Free power, for all his people.'

'Mallard shook his head: 'The trouble is, free power corrupts.'

'What about Badmask?' asked River.

'He's gone. Blown away, and Haig with him,' said Nick.

'That's a relief,' sighed Jem, squeezing Nick's hand.

'It's a double blessing love,' said Mallard. 'And no mistake.'

'What's the matter dad?' asked Jem, detecting a note of hesitation in her father's voice.

Pickup

SHAMI ACTIVATED THE 'CHIP' UNDER HER SKIN AND TOOK SHELTER BY A ROCK.

Wave after wave crashed in and clouds of sea-spray misted her tangled hair. A tear came to her eye, but it didn't get as far as her check. It was River who'd taught her about waves. The rollers always came in sets of twelve. As the last breaker of the sequence washed back out to sea, it deposited an unusual object at her feet. Without thinking, she picked it up to examine it...

In the first *London Deep* adventure...

Jemima Mallard is having a bad day. First she loses her air,
then someone steals her houseboat, and now the Youth Cops
think she's mixed up with a criminal called Father Thames.
Not even her dad, a Chief Inspector with the 'Dult Police, can
help her out this time. Oh – and London's still sinking. It's been
underwater ever since the climate upgrade.

ISBN: 978-1-906132-03-3 £7.99

www.mogzilla.co.uk/londondeep

Chosen as a 'Recommended Read' for World Book Day 2011.
One of the *Manchester Book Award's* 24 recommended titles for. 2010.

MOGZILLA